DANCING WITH DAFFODIL

DANCING WITH DAFFODIL

Al Cunha

INFINITY
PUBLISHING.COM

Copyright © 2009 by Al Cunha

ISBN-13: 978-0-7414-5488-1
ISBN-10: 0-7414-5488-2

Front cover design: Al Cunha and Rose Cunha.

Published by:

INFIƆITY
PUBLISHING.COM

1094 New DeHaven Street, Suite 100
West Conshohocken, PA 19428-2713
Info@buybooksontheweb.com
www.buybooksontheweb.com
Toll-free (877) BUY BOOK
Local Phone (610) 941-9999
Fax (610) 941-9959

Printed in the United States of America
Published 2009; First Edition

To Rose M. Cunha,
my beautiful mother,
my courageous hero.

— and —

To the memory of
Alfred E. Cunha, Sr.,
my wonderful father,
my other hero.

— and —

To all the unfortunate people
who have been left homeless,
extracted from society,
and denied the basic elements of compassion
by those who are more fortunate
and possessing the means to make a difference.

Acknowledgments

To my mother, Rose,
for all the encouragement
she has given to me
while preparing this book for publication.
Many thanks to her,
including a great big thanks
for all the beautiful daffodils
she grew just for me.

To my sister, Diana,
with sincere thanks
for her assistance
during the preparation
of this book for publication.
It was wonderful to have
her help and support.

Many thanks to my readers:
Rachel, Stacy, and Roberta.

"The heart's memory
eliminates the bad
and magnifies the good;
and thanks to this artifice
we manage to endure
the burdens of the past."

—Gabriel Garcia Marquez

DANCING WITH DAFFODIL

Go and get your little red shoes,
Dancing with Daffodil,
Forget about your little-girl blues,
Dancing with Daffodil.

(chorus)
Dance, dance, dance,
Dancing with Daffodil,
Dance, dance, dance,
Dancing with Daffodil.

We'll dance and dance around and around,
Dancing with Daffodil,
We'll dance until the stars fall down,
Dancing with Daffodil.
(repeat chorus)

The music flows in your heart and soul,
Dancing with Daffodil,
Dance and dance and you'll never grow old,
Dancing with Daffodil.
(repeat chorus)

Around and around and around we go,
Dancing with Daffodil,
And when we stop, nobody knows,
Dancing with Daffodil.
(repeat chorus)

Dancing With Daffodil

Words and Music by AL CUNHA

DANCING WITH DAFFODIL

**"Alone in the darkness,
the lonely little girl began to pray."**

PROLOGUE

SAN FRANCISCO BAY AREA

She was only nine years old. How could she fully understand why they took her away from her mother? They were strangers. They were never there when she and her mother would work in the garden together, planting and admiring the daffodils. They were never around when she and her mother would dance and sing to that special song.

In the darkness of the room, curled up in a bed she had never known, she caught a few of the tears that streamed down her face. The images of that horrible morning were still fresh in her mind, scratching at her broken heart. Repeatedly, the painful snapshots of that morning flashed before her. Those last hugs, clinging onto each other, and those kisses that her mother gave her, each one dominated by alcohol, the poison that destroyed their lives, the poison that justified the label of an unfit mother.

The little girl didn't know what to do. She was frightened by her mother's condition, but she didn't want to be taken away by those people she didn't even know. And when she found out that she was being taken away permanently, she begged to stay with her mother, no matter how much her mother had been drinking.

She recalled her mother in front of the house, and the neighbors watching like vultures. She could still see herself gazing through the back window of the car, and through tear-filled eyes, watching her mother curse the people who were taking her daughter from her. She recalled how painful it was when the car pulled away, and how she continued to gaze back through the window until her mother was completely out of sight.

Alone in the darkness, the lonely little girl began to pray.

BORDEAUX, FRANCE

The bicycle had a considerably large basket in front, just past the handlebars. Just above the back fender was another large basket. Both were filled with bread, which had just been baked that morning by the eleven-year-old boy who once again had started out on his favorite mission.

As the young boy continued down the country road, he thought about his dream, which was to own a bakery, and he thought about his good friend, Monsieur Pierre Cousteau.

While pedaling past the trees, he smiled in admiration of the countryside and the presents of spring.

He stopped at the small country church, went inside, and found the priest kneeling at the altar. He knelt down beside him and made the sign of the Cross. The priest did the same. Then he stood up and looked down at the boy. Speaking softly, he told him that he would wait for him outside.

The boy made the sign of the Cross, stood up, and followed the priest out the door.

The priest unwrapped one of the loaves of bread. He was surprised to see the boy's inventory did not include any of the other baked treats, which he usually had to offer. He gave the boy a smile. "Only bread today?" he asked.

"Yes, Father," the boy answered. "It was all that I had time for, but I will have some pastries tomorrow."

"The bread is more than enough, my son. You have done well."

"Thank you, Father."

The priest blessed the bread as the boy bowed his head and silently said a prayer. They ended the blessing and the prayer by making the sign of the Cross together.

"Thank you, Father," the boy said. Then he handed two loaves to the priest.

"Give thanks to God," the priest replied.

"I do, Father."

The priest began walking away. "God be with you, my son," he said.

"And with you, Father."

The boy continued down the road, the loaves of bread blessed, and his spring prayers whispered to God. He stopped along the way as people offered him money and barter for the bread.

His last stop was at a small cottage belonging to Monsieur Pierre Cousteau. The back basket of the bicycle was now filled with bartered items, including milk and cheese, fruit and vegetables, jellies, and candy. In his pocket, there was payment in the form of money.

The front basket had two loaves of bread left. He stopped just in front of the cottage, got off his bicycle, grabbed the bread and carried it with him to the door. His knuckles hit the wood firmly.

Monsieur Cousteau kept to himself, rarely leaving his small cottage. Because he lived like a hermit, many of the neighbors and people in town would talk about him rudely. But to the boy, he was a good friend. Monsieur Cousteau would tell him stories about his life and his travels. They would eat bread and cheese, and they would sip wine and play chess.

The old man's health had been deteriorating for the last few months, and he had complained of chest pains. The boy would help him do things, like making dinner and helping him take his medicine.

The boy continued to knock, but there was no response. Then he opened the door and was shocked by what he saw. On the floor, by the table where the two of them had passed the time by so often, was Monsieur Pierre Cousteau.

The chessboard had been set up, all the pieces in their proper place. Two small glasses of wine had been poured, and there was also a small dish of cheese on the table.

The boy went to the old man's side and looked down at him. "Pierre," the boy whispered. A stream of tears ran down his face.

A relatively short time later after the man had been laid to rest, the boy's family received a letter from an attorney. It informed them that Pierre Cousteau had left the boy a gift. A few days later, the boy and his family met with the attorney in his office.

The attorney went to a cabinet and removed a small wooden box. He put it on his desk, directly in front of the boy.

Slowly, the boy opened it, and his face lit up with surprise as he peered inside at the large amount of money. In addition to the cash was a letter thanking him for his friendship. As he read the letter, tears filled his eyes, a few escaping down his face.

He reached inside and removed a handful of cash. The attorney added that Pierre Cousteau had also left the boy all of his other personal items, including his chess set.

SAN FRANCISCO BAY AREA
(CONCORD)

It was an exciting day for this bright young girl. She was going on a field trip with her seventh-grade class. Although excited, she was somewhat apprehensive about visiting a retirement home. She wondered how she would communicate with the old folks there. She had a great imagination, and several scenarios formed in her mind, including a few intimidating stares, and even an image of one old woman swinging a cane at her.

As the bus came closer to the retirement home, the noise in the bus increased. After the teacher had finally settled the students down, they got off the bus and entered the building.

They went into a large recreation room where several old folks had gathered. After a brief introduction, the children sang songs together. When all the singing was finished, the children walked around, talking with the residents.

Eventually, the girl ended up having a conversation with a lady who was obviously very lonely. She told the girl that her family seldom came to see her, and how much she appreciated the school's visit. She particularly thanked her for her company and the conversation. The loneliness that was nestled in the woman's eyes shot right into the young girl's heart, inspiring her to write.

The girl wrote a poem about her experience with the lady that she had met, and she returned to the retirement home and read it to her. Just her return visit alone would have been enough to bring an abundance of joy to the woman. The poem was a document of how lonely the lady was, and how her family seldom came to visit her.

A short time later, during another visit, the lady told the girl that her family had come to visit her. She explained that when her family read the poem, they all apologized to her. After that, her family came to visit her quite frequently. It made the girl feel so good that her poem had brought so much happiness into the woman's life.

She continued to visit the retirement home, and when the woman passed away, it was a very sad time for that young girl. Two flowers had shared a garden of friendship. When the petals of one grew thin and pale, and finally lost all their color, the other flower blossomed through the sadness and became an aspiring writer. And she would hold the moment in her heart forever.

" 'Sometimes I wish I were a daffodil'."

CHAPTER ONE

A blanket of fog lifted over the city, inviting the arrival of spring on this late morning. The city by the bay was as beautiful as ever. Energy was surging upon the streets as buses and taxis, cars and delivery trucks, and the famous cable cars snaked through the traffic, climbing and descending the renowned hills of San Francisco. Sidewalks and crosswalks were crowded with natives and visitors, shoppers and business people, and the occasional homeless person and panhandler. On the threshold of the twenty-first century, the city had become famous for its culture and its beauty, and it had survived criticism and tragedy.

In an alley, located near the northeast end of Market Street, the business end, was a large cardboard house. To most it would be an eyesore, but to the occupant, it was home.

The towering buildings blocked the sun, denying the alley the core of spring, and instead only casting a residual amount of soft sunlight. Noise from the busy streets funneled into the alley, especially the cars, trucks, and buses, with wheels and brakes squealing, horns honking, and engines accelerating.

Surrounding the cardboard palace was an old card table and four worn-out chairs. Nearby, there was a trash can with a grill on top, and on the grill was a stew pot. There was also a large soup spoon and a ladle on the table.

Another trash can had been turned upside down, and on top was a large flower pot filled with several blooming daffodils. The beautiful yellow flowers were in direct contrast with the surroundings, but that only held true in the absence of their admiring creator.

An old piece of plywood had been set upon a stack of four worn-out car tires. Flower pots, gardening tools, and a large garbage bag filled with aluminum cans were on that piece of plywood. Sharing that space were other belongings, including books, magazines, knickknacks, a few small boxes, as well as a few other miscellaneous items. There were also cooking pots, bowls, dishes, and eating utensils on the card table, and nearby was a broom.

A large intimidating figure entered the west end of the alley. He was tall and broad, dressed in his police uniform. His stride was steady, his feet hitting the pavement firmly. He passed by the back of Eddie Chan's Chinese Restaurant and a dumpster, and as he continued, he passed another dumpster and garbage cans. His face reflected the haunting thoughts that occupied his mind. His eyes were cold and calculating as he walked toward the castle of cardboard, which was located about halfway down the alley.

Upon reaching the homeless establishment that he knew so well, he grabbed his nightstick and struck the cardboard house, then continued to pound all over the structure.

"Maggie!" he bellowed. "Maggie, come on out of there!"

From inside the cardboard house, Maggie replied with her feisty voice. "What the hell is going on?" she asked.

"Come on, Maggie. I haven't got all day."

"Yeah, yeah! Just hold onto your shorts, McGuinness!"

"That's *Officer* McGuinness," he corrected.

Maggie poked her head out. Her eyes were fearless, her smile carefree. "All right," she said, "hold onto your shorts, *Officer* McGuinness." He watched with frustration as she crawled her way out of the cardboard palace and stood up. The printed flowers on her slightly tattered dress were faded, and the old beat-up shoes seemed to match the long strands of her shaggy, uncombed hair. "You should be ashamed of yourself," she taunted, "disturbing people when they're sleeping."

He shook his nightstick at her. "Look, Maggie, I've told you a thousand times now. I want you and your box out of this alley."

"This is not a box!" she snapped, pointing to the cardboard house. "It's my house—my home. It's where I live. Get it?"

"Well, I'm sorry, Maggie, but you're going to have to take your house, and all this other crap, and move it somewhere else. Now I don't want any more arguing about it. You have to get out of here. I've got my orders."

"Orders? Orders from who?"

"Come on, Maggie, it doesn't make any difference."

"The hell it doesn't. Now I want to know where your stupid orders come from."

"My orders come from the chief."

Her eyes were filled with defiance. "Oh yeah?" she replied. "Then you tell *him* to come down here and talk to me."

"In your dreams, Maggie."

"No, not in my dreams. Right here. You tell your high and mighty chief to come down here and talk to me."

"I don't think so, Maggie."

"Why not?" she asked, anxious for an answer.

"Because he's the chief of police, that's why," he said. "It's not his job to do that. It's mine."

"What, your farts don't stink as bad as his, or what?" she replied abrasively.

"You sure are one feisty lady."

She gave him an angry look. "Yeah, and you're making me one *pissed-off* lady."

Flashes of his past shot through his mind, and reflections of a tragedy turned into anger burning on his face, and driving in his voice. "You know, Maggie," he said, "I think you ought to have a little more respect for an officer of the law."

"Why? You don't have any respect for me, so there."

"You just get your box, and all your crap, and get out of this alley," he said, looking around at the cardboard house and her belongings.

"When roosters lay eggs!" she quickly shot back. "Like I said, I want your chief to come down here and talk to me himself."

"Damn it, I told you, Maggie—that's my job."

"Yeah, well you tell me something else, McGuinness. Why does the chief want me out of here so bad, anyway?"

"Because he's got *his* orders, that's why."

"*His* orders?"

"That's right. He's got his orders from higher up."

"Higher up?"

"That's right. The mayor told him to clean up the city."

"Oh yeah?" she snapped. "Then you tell the mayor to get *his* fancy ass down here."

"I don't think so, Maggie."

"Why not?"

"Because he's got more important things to do," he said, glancing around the immediate area, "and so does the chief, and as a matter of fact, so do I. Now I've got to be moving along."

"McGuinness, I'm not getting out of here until I talk to either the chief of police or the mayor."

"First of all, that will never happen. Second of all, it wouldn't do any good, anyway."

"You don't know that, McGuinness." She replied. As she continued, the words rolled out of her mouth in a smooth, logical flow. "If I explain to them how this is my home, maybe they'll understand, and then I wouldn't have to leave."

"Look, Maggie," he said, continuing to glance at the cardboard house and the other items around him, "this place might be home to you, but to the city, it's an eyesore."

Maggie's voice was coated with sadness. "Yeah, I know, but it's all I've got. I've been here for almost a year now." She glanced at the cardboard house, then she looked deeply into his eyes. "It's my home, you know?" she said.

His voice swelled with authority as he glared straight at her. "I'm sorry, Maggie," he said firmly, "but I've got my orders. I've got to be moving along now. I'll talk to you later."

A tornado of tension swirled inside her as she watched him walk away toward the east end of the alley. Then she began to calm down as her mind drifted into thoughts that took her to another time, then on a path back to the present, and a look through her eyes at her life in the alley.

Maggie May Salokavich had told her story, not only to everyone she knew and didn't know, but she had also told it to her daffodils.

She would describe herself as a Slavonian drop-out—a drop-out from life. She would say that she had everything—a nice house, a nice car, good friends, and most of all, a wonderful family—a wonderful husband, and the sweetest little girl in the world—Daffodil. And she blamed herself for what happened.

She had lived in the alley for almost a whole year, and to her it was home. Before that, she would just curl up in an old ragged blanket underneath a bridge, and before that—another alley. And prior to that, her shelter consisted of some sticks and a tarp by the dump. She liked to tell everyone about how badly it would stink.

The first night that Maggie was on the street, she slept down by the wharf. It was cold and foggy, and she felt that she had been exiled from a world that no longer accepted her as a normal human being. She felt as if she were on the outside looking in, wanting to scream out at everyone, to warn them.

She wanted to just yell out, "One more bottle, and you could be here with me! One more unpaid mortgage payment, or rent payment, and you could be here with me." But then she thought there would be no use in doing that because they wouldn't listen anyway.

Where she was now had become her home, and she had said many times that nobody was going to kick Maggie May Salokavich out of her house—nobody.

Spring was Maggie's favorite season because that was when her daffodils would bloom. The daffodils were more than just flowers to her. They were her friends, and they were her memories, the memories that blossomed year round in her heart, her mind, and her soul.

She went back into the cardboard house and came out with a wine bottle filled with water. She approached the daffodils and began to speak to them. "Are you thirsty?" she asked. She poured some water in the flower pot. "There you go," she continued. "Don't worry, it's just water. Well, to be perfectly honest with you, there was a little wine left in it. But what the hell, you're all kings, right? King Alfred—king of the daffodils. All kings like wine, don't they? Sure they do. You're all lucky to be daffodils. Sometimes I wish I were a daffodil." Then she went back inside her cardboard house.

From the west end of the alley, a man in white appeared. The only thing that was missing from his attire was his matching white hat. Not only was he a baker, but he also owned and ran the bakery, which was located nearby. Maurice Bonné was a handsome man of twenty-seven, always giving everyone a friendly smile and a gentle gleam of kindness in his eyes. He had become a fairly good businessman, and because he had always been a generous person, he gave something back to people whenever he could.

People came to his bakery, not only for the donuts and other pastries, and not only because everyone liked him, but they also came to listen to his French accent.

Carrying a cup of coffee and a bag of donuts, he walked by the back of Eddie Chan's Chinese Restaurant. He glanced at the graffiti on the dumpster and the garbage cans. Continuing down the alley toward the cardboard palace, he thought about his friendship with Maggie, and that alone brought a smile to his gentle face. Then, as he stood there in front of Maggie's house, his smile grew with a sense of pride, for he valued something that many people would never understand—his friendship with a homeless woman.

Maurice placed the cup of coffee on the table. He then began knocking on the cardboard house.

From inside came a familiar voice, which was not friendly at all. "McGuinness, you ol' fuzzball," she yelled out, "is that you again?"

"No, Maggie, it is me—Maurice—Frenchy."

Maggie poked her head out of the cardboard house. "Well, hell, why didn't you say so, Frenchy?"

Retaining his smile, Maurice watched as she came out of her house. "I brought you some donuts and coffee, Maggie," he said, handing her the coffee and donuts.

"Frenchy, you're too good to me."

"Well, you need someone to be good to you."

"People *are* good to me. It's just fate that's been a bastard."

"Speaking of bastards, I want to thank you again for helping me catch that thief the other day. You were magnificent."

Maggie peered into the bag, then she removed a donut. "No problem," she said. "Anything for my ol' pal Frenchy."

Maurice laughed. "You know, I will never forget that guy flying over those empty garbage cans," he said.

Maggie responded as she continued to eat the donut. "Yeah," she replied, "he sure did go flipity-flop, didn't he?"

"Flipity-flop and crash-bang. I would have never caught him if you wouldn't have rolled those empty garbage cans out in front of him. I must say, those policemen were very impressed."

"Yeah, I wish ol' fuzzball McGuinness could have been here."

"Well, *you* were here, and I will never forget it."

Sipping her coffee, Maggie thought about what Maurice had done for her. "Yeah, well," she said, "*you* were here when I needed somebody. I'll never forget how hungry I was the day that I first met you. The pain in my stomach was horrible."

"Oui, Maggie, I remember that well. I could see the hunger on your face."

There was a proud smile on her face as she recalled the day. "I'll never forget how you went back to your bakery, and then came back with a bag full of donuts, just like the ones you brought me today, and a cup of coffee, just like this one."

"You know that guy ordered two dozen donuts, then just ran out of my bakery. Of course, he had no idea that Maggie May Salokavich would be there to stop him with the garbage cans."

With laughter, Maggie recalled the incident. "What I remember most of all is all those donuts flying all over the place."

There was a serious tone in Maurice's voice. "You know, Maggie," he said, "the whole world should be like you and me—helping each other out. It would be a much better place, wouldn't it?"

Maggie took another donut out of the bag. "It'll never happen, Frenchy."

"I know, but I sure do wish that it could."

"Yeah, well, wish in one hand, and shit in the other. See which one gets the fullest."

"You sure are something, Maggie. You are certainly a work of art. You know, this alley would never be the same without you."

Maggie thought about Officer McGuinness's visit earlier, and her thoughts echoed into a serious expression upon her face. "Well, if that ol' fuzzball McGuinness gets his way, I won't be here too much longer," she said.

"Did he come by again?"

"Yeah. I told him I wanted the chief of police or the mayor to come down here and talk to me, because I'm not leaving."

With a chuckle, Maurice looked at her proudly. "Like I said, you sure are something, Maggie."

"Ol' fuzzball McGuinness called me feisty."

"I must admit, he is right about that."

A part of Maggie's heart and soul was reflecting in her eyes as she spoke. "Yeah, well," she said, "when you're on the streets, you learn to be feisty. You have to be feisty and assertive, or you don't survive. And that's what it's all about, Frenchy—survival."

" '…She's the song that I hear,
the song that I sing.
She's the beauty that I see.
She's the dance that I dance.
She's my golden trumpet,
so very precious,
and more beautiful
than even Queen Anne.
She's Daffodil—
my sweet little Daffodil'."

CHAPTER TWO

Sounds from the city funneled into the alley throughout the night. They were much more shallow than the ones during the day, and they were not as frequent. The fragments of conversations that drifted through the alley during the day were also gone. They were replaced by the monstrous sound of a passing street cleaner and the loud engines and huge iron arms of the garbage trucks, the sound of the banging metal of dumpsters being lifted, emptied, and wheeled back to where they were. Cats fighting and mating, drunks moaning and falling on empty garbage cans, and the sound of shattered glass from bottles being tossed to the ground filled the darkness of the foggy night.

But now the darkness had given way to the light of the morning. Another spring day had arrived. The fog had already lifted, and Maggie felt good about surviving another night in the alley. She was still alive, and maybe not part of what most people would call normal society, but she was still part of the world. She could still talk to other homeless people, whether she knew them or not, and she felt proud to have a friend like Maurice.

She could still sing and dance, and surround herself with memories. And she had her daffodils. She could talk to them, and they would listen. But what she was especially thankful for was that she could still dance with Daffodil.

Maggie used a large spoon to stir the stew. She made large circles with it, extending them almost all the way to the inside perimeter of the stew pot. As she continued to stir, she hummed the chorus of *Dancing With Daffodil*, a song that she sang every day. She sprinkled some salt and pepper into the pot.

She filled a ladle with a small amount of stew and put it in a small bowl, and then sampled it. "Mmmm, good," she said, "but not quite right yet." Realizing that it needed a little more of something, she grabbed a bottle of wine and poured some into the pot. Again, she put some stew in the bowl and gave it another taste, bringing a smile of satisfaction. "Mmmm, now that's what I call sunshine stew," she said. "Much, much better."

Now satisfied that she had once again brought perfection to her sunshine stew, she began to dance, holding her arms out in front of her, holding the hands of an imaginary child. Then she began to sing.

"Dance, dance, dance,
Dancing with Daffodil,
Dance, dance, dance,
Dancing with Daffodil."

Although surprised to see a beautiful young woman approaching, she continued to sing and dance without allowing herself to be interrupted. Even though she did continue, her curiosity would not escape her. She wondered what a beautiful young woman, dressed in a chic top, skirt, and coat would be doing in an alley. The woman continued to walk down the alley toward her, then just stood there smiling, listening to her song, watching her dance, amazed by her hands holding onto a child who wasn't there.

"Go and get your little red shoes,
Dancing with Daffodil,
Forget about your little-girl blues,
Dancing with Daffodil.

"Dance, dance, dance,
Dancing with Daffodil,
Dance, dance, dance,
Dancing with Daffodil.

"We'll dance and dance around and around,
Dancing with Daffodil,
We'll dance until the stars fall down,
Dancing with Daffodil.

"Dance, dance, dance,
Dancing with Daffodil,
Dance, dance, dance,
Dancing with Daffodil.

"The music flows in your heart and soul,
Dancing with Daffodil,
Dance and dance and you'll never grow old,
Dancing with Daffodil.

"Dance, dance, dance,
Dancing with Daffodil,
Dance, dance, dance,
Dancing with Daffodil.

"Around and around and around we go,
Dancing with Daffodil,
And when we stop, nobody knows,
Dancing with Daffodil.

"Dance, dance, dance,
Dancing with Daffodil,
Dance, dance, dance,
Dancing with Daffodil."

Maggie gave the woman a friendly smile. "Hello," she said.

"Hello. That's a pretty song you were singing."

"Thank you," she replied proudly. "I wrote it myself."

"Well, that's very impressive."

"Thank you. I wrote it for Daffodil. That's who I was dancing with."

The young woman played along. "Oh, really? And who is Daffodil?" she asked.

"Daffodil is the prettiest, sweetest little girl in the whole world. That's who she is."

The young woman came to a conclusion that she considered to be obvious. "She must be your daughter," she said.

"Daffodil is Daffodil. She's the aching in my heart. She's the fabric that holds me together. Without her memory, my tattered life would completely unravel. There would be only threads of heartbreak—threads of misery."

Even though the young woman felt sure that Maggie was talking about her daughter, she felt the need for confirmation. "But Daffodil *is* your daughter, isn't she?" she asked.

But again, without any real confirming words, she just looked at the young woman and smiled proudly, allowing the words to pour from her heart and tear away from her soul. "Daffodil is Daffodil," Maggie began to explain again. "She's the song that I hear, the song that I sing. She's the beauty that I see. She's the dance that I dance. She's my golden trumpet, so very precious, and more beautiful than even Queen Anne. She's Daffodil—my sweet little Daffodil."

Realizing that she might not get a confirming word from this homeless woman, she allowed the natural flow of her professional duties to take over. "How long have you been homeless?" she asked.

The look on Maggie's face was one that indicated she had no clue to how the young woman could have ever gotten the idea that she was homeless. "Homeless?" she replied. "Homeless? I'm not homeless." She pointed briefly to the cardboard condo. "I've got a home right here," she said. "I must admit, it doesn't have running water and central heating, or a microwave, or a real stove, or a dishwasher, or a garbage disposal, or a lot of fancy furniture. But I do have my house. It's my house. The bank doesn't own it. It's all mine, Fancy Pants—all mine. And you know what? I don't have to pay any taxes on it either. And you know what else? I don't have any bills."

She thought about being homeless while she stirred the stew. "You see, Fancy Pants," she continued, "I'm my own person, and I live in my own little world. Homeless? No, I'm not homeless. I'm a lost soul in a world of lost compassion."

The young woman didn't know quite how to respond, which made her feel a bit awkward, because that was part of her job. For a moment, she allowed her mind to digest Maggie's words as she watched her make circles in the stew.

Curiosity swept across Maggie's face as she looked at the young woman. "So what are you doing around here, anyway?" she asked. "I know you're not here to sample my sunshine stew, although it is pretty tasty."

"I'm a writer. I'm doing a story on the homeless."

"Well, then you're in the wrong place, because I told you, I'm not homeless. I'm only a lost soul in a world of lost compassion."

The young woman knew it would be of no use to argue with her. "Yes, of course," she replied. "What's your name?"

"Maggie—Maggie May Salokavich. What's yours?"

"Della—Della Houston. Maggie, would you mind if I interviewed you?"

"Naw, hell, I don't care. How about some sunshine stew? I've got lots of goodies in there— lots of garlic."

Della wondered what other things might be inside the pot besides just garlic, what other things that she might not even consider as food. "Oh, no thanks," she replied politely.

Maggie made it clear that she was offended. "What," she said, "you too good for my stew?"

"No, of course not."

"Then, damn it, have some stew."

"I'm really not hungry."

"You don't know what you're missing, Fancy Pants."

Della looked into the pot, scrutinizing the stew. "That's Della," she said, not taking her eyes off the stew.

Maggie quickly gazed into the stew along with her. "No, that's stew," she replied. "*You're* Della. Remember?"

They both took their attention away from the stew pot. "That's very humorous," Della said.

"Hell, the only thing humorous around here was one time when Eddie Chan came out of his restaurant, just down the alley there," she said, pointing briefly to the place down the alley. "He was just about to throw some garbage in the dumpster. Boy, did he ever get a surprise. Mr. Rummy came by and jumped on him. Eddie lost his balance and fell down."

Maggie definitely had Della's attention. "Mr. Rummy jumped on him?" she asked.

"Yeah, you should have seen him. He had rice, and chow mein, and noodles, and sauce all over him. And the funniest thing was, Mr. Rummy was licking all that stuff off his face. I just laughed and laughed and laughed."

"Well, I don't know what's so funny about that," Della replied. "I'd say that was very cruel of that Mr. Rummy to do something like that. And to lick the garbage off that poor man's face—well, I can hardly believe any man would do something so—so—so sick."

Maggie was amused. "Mr. Rummy isn't a man," she said. "He's a cat."

"A cat? Oh yeah, of course—a cat."

"That's right, Fancy Pants."

"I'm Della. My name is Della."

"Yeah, I know."

"Well, then why do you call me Fancy Pants?"

"Hell, I don't know. You just look like a Fancy Pants. Hell, I can't explain it. I can't analyze it."

Della took a writing tablet and a pen out of her purse. "So, tell me more about Daffodil," she said.

"Look, before we have this little interview, you've got to taste my sunshine stew."

Once again, Della thought about what might be in the stew. Her imagination began to run wild, bringing images that included stray cats and insects. "I really couldn't."

"Oh yes you could."

"No, I really couldn't."

"Then neither could I. No stew—no interview." She was amused by her own words. "Hey, that rhymes," she said laughing. "I'm a poet and I didn't even know it."

Officer McGuinness was approaching them in the very near distance. "I smell sunshine stew," he bellowed.

"And I smell a fuzzball," Maggie replied.

Officer McGuinness took a good look at Della. "Who's your friend, Maggie?" he asked.

"Oh, you mean Fancy Pants?"

Della was embarrassed by the name that she was introduced with, and that caused a bit of anger to swell up inside her. "I am not Fancy Pants!" she said, giving Maggie a scolding look. Then she directed her attention to Officer McGuinness to correct the false introduction. "My name is Della Houston," she said, making it perfectly clear. "I'm a writer."

To Della's surprise, the officer took advantage of the situation so that he could tease her. "Fancy Pants, huh?" he teased.

Della gave Maggie another scolding gaze. "Thanks a lot, Maggie," she said.

"No problem."

The officer continued to tease her. "So, Fancy Pants, are you one of those starving writers?" he asked.

Maggie answered for her. "Hell no," she said. "She can't be starving, or she would have jumped at the chance to have some of my sunshine stew."

Officer McGuinness had a serious look upon his face. "You know, Fancy Pants," he said, "maybe you can talk some sense into this woman."

Della didn't feel comfortable with the way the officer was speaking to her, the way he was teasing her, and the way he was beginning to attack a defenseless homeless woman.

"First of all," she said, "I would appreciate it if you would quit calling me Fancy Pants. My name is Della, and I'm here to conduct an interview."

"She's doing a story on homeless people," Maggie said. "I told her I'm not homeless." She pointed briefly to her cardboard condo. "I've got my home right here."

"Not for long, Maggie," the officer sneered.

"McGuinness, you ol' fuzzball, you've been telling me that for the last six months."

"I'm sorry, Maggie, but I just got the word this morning. You've got two weeks to stay here. That's it—two weeks. If you're still here at that time, they're just going to show up and tear down your cardboard palace. And they'll get rid of everything else, including you."

"But why would anyone want to do that?" Della replied in Maggie's defense. "She's not hurting anybody."

"You tell him, Fancy Pants!" Maggie said.

The officer directed his words in a clear, stern voice. "Two weeks, Maggie," he warned. "Two weeks." Then, as he began walking away, he gave a threatening gaze at Della. "And you better watch your step, Fancy Pants," he said, directing his words straight into her eyes. "I'm warning you. Stay out of my way." Della said nothing as he walked away, heading toward the east end of the alley.

"Fuzzball!" Maggie yelled, as she watched the officer walk away. There was a smile of gratitude on her face as she looked at Della. "Thank you for what you said."

"Well, I think it's just terrible ."

Della noticed a man coming down the alley. There was a smile on his face, and a loaf of French bread in his hand. He was dressed in his white baking attire, but without the hat.

"Mmmmm mmm, I smell sunshine stew," Maurice said as he approached them.

"Hey, Frenchy, what's rising?" Maggie greeted.

"I brought you some bread for your stew."

"Thanks. That was real nice of you."

Maurice tried not to show the attraction that he felt as he looked at Della. He spoke, not taking his eyes off her. "I see you have company," he said.

"Oh, this is Della," Maggie said. "And this is Frenchy—I mean, Maurice—Maurice Bonné. He owns a bakery, just down at the next alley."

"Hello, Maurice," Della said, shaking his hand.

"Bonjour, Della."

Della felt an equal attraction to him, and she tried her best to hide it.

"She's a writer," Maggie said.

"Oh, that is nice—very nice. What do you write?"

"Right now, I'm working on assignment for World Status Magazine. I'm doing an article on the homeless."

"I told her I'm not homeless," Maggie said. She pointed to her cardboard house. "I've got my home right here."

"Yes, but not for long," Della reminded her.

Maggie looked at Maurice with angry eyes. "That ol' Fuzzball McGuinness just came by again," she said. "He told me in two weeks, the city's going to chase me out of here."

"They should be ashamed of themselves," he said.

Della was focused on Maurice. "I agree," she replied. "I think it's just terrible."

"Oui, it sure is. You know, I would like to stay and talk, but I have a lot of work to do." He gave Maggie a comforting smile. "Do not let it bring you down, Maggie," he said. "Gardez la foi. Gardez la foi."

"What does that mean?" Maggie asked.

"Keep the faith, Maggie. Keep the faith. Now I must go."

"Thanks for the bread, Frenchy."

"No problem. It is my pleasure." He felt his heart beating a little faster as he looked at Della. "It was very nice to meet you, Della," he said.

The filter that he was trying to apply to his feelings was becoming weaker, and she could read the expression on his face. Even more obvious was the unmistakable look she was giving him.

"It was nice to meet you too, Maurice."

"Au revoir," he said.

"Bye."

"See you later, Frenchy."

"Au revoir."

Della kept her focus on Maurice as he walked away, headed down the alley, back to his bakery. An unmistakable smile remained on her face.

Maggie was amused by Della's attraction to Maurice. "Look at you," she teased. "You're all ga-ga."

"All ga-ga? What do you mean?" she asked, knowing exactly what she meant.

"You know perfectly well what I mean. I saw the way you looked at Maurice."

"Was it that obvious?"

"Like a big fart in a small church."

"You certainly have a way with words, don't you?"

"I don't know. I can't analyze it. Look, Fancy Pants, if you want that interview—well, it's yours."

"Thanks, Maggie. I appreciate that." She looked over at the stew pot. "You know, I think I will take a bowl of that stew," she said.

A big smile quickly swept across Maggie's face. "You got it, Fancy Pants." She said. "One bowl of Maggie May's sunshine stew comin' up."

" '…I loved daffodils so much.
I could hardly wait for them
to bloom each season…'."

CHAPTER THREE

To Della's surprise, Maggie's sunshine stew had turned out to be very good. She had asked her some questions about her life as they enjoyed the meal. Like Maggie, she would dip the bread into the stew, and when she was finished, she cleaned the bowl with it. During her conversation with Maggie, she thought of Maurice.

They were sitting at the card table. Della was flipping through some pages of her writing tablet. She looked across the table at Maggie. "Let me just confirm a few things," she said. "Your grandparents, both on your mother's side and your father's side, came from Czechoslovakia. After coming to the United States, they came to California and settled in Watsonville. Is that correct?"

"That's right."

Della continued to review her notes, turning the pages of the tablet. "Your mother and father were born and raised in Watsonville. Then *you* were also born and raised there. Is that correct?"

"You got it."

"Your maiden name is Velkovich. Your father's name is Daniel, and your mother's name is Mary. Is all this correct?"

"You're doing real good, Fancy Pants."

Della gave her an irritated look because of the repeated use of the nickname Maggie had chosen for her. "You met your husband, Sam, in Santa Cruz, on the boardwalk," she continued. "He had just graduated from college. Then after his graduate work here in San Francisco, you were married. Then he took a job as an accountant. Is that correct?"

"You got it, Fancy Pants."

There was a stern look on Della's face. "My name is Della," she said, "not Fancy Pants."

"Yeah, I know."

Eager to go on with the interview, Della quickly decided to let the matter go for the moment. "So Daffodil was nine years old when they took her away from you. Correct?"

"Correct."

"And it's been about fifteen years since you've seen her? Is that right?"

"That's right."

"And you're forty-four years old. Right?"

"No, I'm forty-four years young, Fancy Pants."

"Okay—forty-four years young."

"I won't ever get old," Maggie said, "not as long as I have my memories of Daffodil. Besides, age is only a number. It might change the direction that you're going, but it will never change where you've already been. It can change your face, but it will never change who you are."

Della captured Maggie's words and held onto them, savoring the sweet philosophy, recognizing the profound truth. "I'd like to quote you on that," she said.

"Sure. Why not? So how old are *you*, Fancy Pants?"

"Della," she replied, filling her writing tablet with more notes. "My name is Della."

"Okay. How old are you, Della?" Maggie asked again.

"Twenty-four."

"Just a little spring chicken," Maggie said.

Della had immersed herself in the confirmation of her notes too much to respond to Maggie's teasing remark. "And the song that you wrote— *Dancing With Daffodil*—you said that your husband's sister-in-law recorded it."

"That's right."

"So she was married to your husband's brother?"

"Yeah, that's right. Her name is Natassia. She and some of her friends recorded it and gave it to Daffodil on her sixth birthday."

"Do you know where she's at now?"

"You mean Natassia?"

"Yeah."

"Naw, heck, I don't know where anybody's at," Maggie replied. "I haven't talked to anyone since I've been out on the street."

"How about your parents?"

There was a sad look on Maggie's face. "They're both in heaven," she said.

"Oh, I'm sorry. Now, let's see…" She put the writing tablet down and removed a microcassette tape recorder from her purse. "Maggie, would you mind if I used this?"

"Naw, hell, I don't care."

"Thank you." She pressed the buttons on the tape recorder to begin recording. Even though she was now using the tape recorder, she picked up the tablet and continued writing. "So what happened between the time you got married and moved to San Francisco, and now?" she asked.

"In twenty-five words or less?" Maggie joked.

That brought a chuckle from Della. "I'm sure it's going to require more than twenty-five words," she said.

"Two years after Sam and I were married, we had a baby. We were so happy. I loved daffodils so much. I could hardly wait for them to bloom each season. That's the way it was when I was pregnant with my daughter. It was like waiting for a daffodil to bloom. I told my husband that, and he said, 'Well maybe we should name the baby Daffodil if it's a girl.' So we did. We named her Daffodil."

"That's a beautiful name," Della said.

"She was a beautiful little girl," Maggie replied.

"Where is she now?"

"I don't know."

"Why don't you know?"

Maggie avoided Della's question. Instead, she continued with her memories of Daffodil, directed to herself more than Della, more from her heart than her mind. "She was a beautiful little girl—such a little sweetheart. My sweet little Daffodil. She just loved to dance. I'd be working in my garden, and she would come out and talk to me. She would always want me to dance with her. She would say, 'Mommy, dance with me—dance with me. Please.' And I would always say, 'Okay, go and get your little red shoes.' How she loved those little red shoes. She would put on the music, and we'd dance and dance and dance."

A smile grew upon Maggie's face as she began to dance around, pretending to be dancing with Daffodil. She held her arms out in front of her, holding onto the hands of the little girl who wasn't really there. Maggie looked down and gave the imaginary little girl a big sustaining smile. Then she began to sing as she continued to dance.

"Go and get your little red shoes,
Dancing with Daffodil,
Forget about your little-girl blues,
Dancing with Daffodil.

"Dance, dance, dance,
Dancing with Daffodil,
Dance, dance, dance,
Dancing with Daffodil.

"We'll dance and dance around and around,
Dancing with Daffodil,
We'll dance until the stars fall down,
Dancing with Daffodil.

"Dance, dance, dance,
Dancing with Da..."

She was abruptly interrupted as the boisterous voice of Officer McGuinness silenced the chorus of her special song. "Maggie," he said roughly. "Maggie, you better quit all this singing and dancing around. You get all your crap together, and get the hell out of here."

A surge of anger swelled up inside Della, and she looked at Officer McGuinness, a look of disbelief upon her face. "That's no way to talk to her," she said. "You leave her alone."

"Yeah, that's no way to talk to me, you freakin' fuzzball," Maggie said.

"You should have a little more respect for the law, Maggie," he said. Then he turned his attention to Della. "And so should you," he added.

Della had come to the alley to make some conversation with a homeless person, get a few notes, and then leave with a story. The possibility of becoming swept up into an emotional whirlwind never came to her mind. But that's exactly what was happening. She felt compelled to fight for the cause of this woman, to stand by her and help defend her. "Well, I'm sorry," she said, "but it's a little difficult to pay you any respect after you talk like that to

Maggie. Now, unless you'd like me to report you in for harassment, I'd like you to leave so I can continue my interview."

"Yeah, well you can put this in your story," he said ruthlessly. "Officer Tim McGuinness will be cleaning up this alley, and he's going to be sweeping away all the bums, just like Maggie."

It was an insult that quickly pinched a nerve, and Maggie echoed that in her response. "You ol' fuzzball!" she replied. "I'm not a bum!"

He found only amusement in her reply. "Oh, well excuse me," he said sarcastically. "I didn't mean to insult such an outstanding citizen."

"McGuinness, you freakin' fuzzball, why don't you just go and bother somebody else?" Maggie snapped.

"Why are you harassing her?" Della asked.

"I'm just doing my job, that's all," he said. Then, sternly, with cold eyes, he looked at Maggie. "I've got to be on my way now, Maggie. Just remember," he warned, "you've got two weeks. That's it, Maggie—two weeks." Then he looked at Della and pronounced his words slowly and precisely so that she could understand his warning. "And you better watch your step, young lady," he said. His words lingered in his eyes.

Della said nothing. She just looked at him with disgust. Then he walked away, heading down the alley toward the east end.

"Freakin' fuzzball!" Maggie called out to him.

"I've never seen a police officer act so rudely," Della said. "It seems like there's always one bad apple in every bunch."

"You know, I used to pick apples in Watsonville," Maggie said. "I used to pick berries, too. That was a long time ago. You like apples, Fancy Pants?"

"Do I like apples?"

"Oh, I'm sorry, Alex, let's try another category. It sounds like that one is way too difficult."

"Very funny."

"Well, do you like apples or don't you?" Maggie asked again.

"Yes, Maggie, I like apples."

"How about berries? You like berries, Fancy Pants?"

"Yes, I like berries, and it's Della."

"You like strawberries?"

"Yes, I like strawberries."

"How about raspberries? You like raspberries?"

Della was eager to continue the interview, and all the questions about apples and berries were starting to make her a little frustrated, and her replies were peppered with sighs. "Yes, Maggie," she replied, "I like raspberries."

"How about blackberries?" Maggie continued. "You like blackberries?"

"Yes, I like blackberries. Now could we please continue the interview?"

"Go for it, Fancy Pants."

"Thank you, Maggie—and my name is Della."

"Yeah, I know."

Della began looking at her notes. "Now let's see…"

"How about boysenberries?" Maggie continued. "You like boysenberries?"

"Yes, I like boysenberries. Now, Maggie, I really would like to continue with…"

"So what's your favorite—red apples or green apples?" she asked, interrupting.

Della tried to hide her growing frustration. "Maggie, could we just forget about the berries, and the apples?"

"I could never forget that," Maggie replied quickly, "especially the apples. The apple orchard is where I first kissed a boy. I'll never forget that, sitting there underneath that apple tree, giving each other innocent little kisses, eating apples, streams of sunlight filtering through the orchard. It was a beautiful age of innocence." She conveyed a teasing smile to Della. "How about you, Fancy Pants?" she asked. "Where were you the first time you kissed a boy?"

"Maggie, who's conducting this interview—me or you?"

"I don't know? Who cares? So where were you? Where were you the first time you kissed a boy?"

"I'm sorry, Maggie. I really can't remember."

"Oh, that's a shame. Those kind of memories are so precious."

"Yes, I agree, but I think we should continue with the interview."

"Where were you the first time you made love?" Maggie continued. "I bet you remember that, don't you?"

There was nothing Della could do to stop the images from flashing through her mind. "Maggie, I really do need to finish this interview, so could we please forget about *my* life, and concentrate on yours?"

"Go for it, Fancy Pants."

"Thank you, and my name is Della. Now, Maggie, why is it that you don't know where your daughter is?"

"I had such a wonderful life," Maggie replied, avoiding the question. "It was more than I could ever wish for. Then my husband got very sick, and then, like I told you, he passed away."

"That must have been very difficult for you."

"After that, I started drinking—drinking a lot. As time went on, it just got worse and worse. I was out of control. Then someone reported me in and said that I was an alcoholic, and they said that I was an unfit mother, and they were right."

"And is that when they took your daughter away?"

"Yes, that's when they took her away."

"And how do you feel about that?"

"At the time, I thought it was wrong."

"And now?"

"Now I know they were just trying to protect Daffodil. I was out of control. I know she still loves me. I tried to give Daffodil her little red shoes, but she didn't want them anymore. She said she only wanted them if—if she could 'dance with Mommy.' I gave the shoes away—all of them—every red pair she had ever worn."

"Why did you do that?"

"Because being an alcoholic caused me to lose Daffodil, and I hated myself for that. My heart was broken, and so was my mind. I ended up in a mental hospital. I knew that I would probably be there for a long time.

"Then I found out that Daffodil was adopted by a couple who eventually moved somewhere in the Midwest. I realized that my chances of ever seeing Daffodil again were not very good. So anyway, I got rid of those little red shoes, because it just hurt too much to look at them. I got rid of the music, too."

A blanket of emotion wrapped tightly around Della. It was more than just a story for a magazine now. It was much more. She felt herself attached to this homeless soul. "How terribly sad," she said.

"I can still see Daffodil, the tears spilling from her eyes. I can still hear her pleading with the authorities who took her away." A tear ran down Maggie's face as she began to cry. " 'No, Mommy! No, Mommy! No, Mommy! Mommy, please don't let them take me! Please don't let them take me'!" And then she could talk no more as tears spilled from her eyes.

Della put her arms around Maggie, trying to comfort her. She had come to the alley to get an interview, but instead she found herself becoming a part of this woman's life, her fight for dignity, her memories, and her sadness. She continued to hold

Maggie in her arms the same way that she might do with her own mother. She felt something beating. Was it her heart, or was it Maggie's, or was it both? A teardrop escaped as Della blinked.

"The passion that pulsed
in their hearts
was echoed in the sparkles
dancing in their eyes."

CHAPTER FOUR

Almost two weeks had passed. According to Officer McGuinness, it was to be the last day that Maggie would be allowed to stay in the alley. But she was not busy getting her things together. She wasn't anywhere in the alley, and it was much too late in the day for her to be in the cardboard house.

Della had just parked her car, and she was now headed to see Maggie. There was a satisfied smile on her face as she came near her destination. When she entered the east end of the alley, she felt herself becoming increasingly anxious to give Maggie some good news. As she began walking down the alley, Maurice was approaching the west end.

Della was surprised when she found that Maggie was not anywhere to be seen. She knew it was possible that she could be inside the cardboard house, but she realized it was not like Maggie to be inside so late in the day.

She stepped over to the cardboard house. "Maggie?" she called. "Maggie, are you in there?" But there was no answer. She bent down a little, trying to peek inside. "Maggie, I've got good news for you. Maggie?" But instead of a voice from the cardboard house, there was one that came as a surprise behind her.

"Bonjour, Della," Maurice greeted.

"Oh, hi, Maurice. How are you?"

"Very good, thank you. And you?"

The curious expression on her face was quickly swept away by one of smiling satisfaction. "I am just great, Maurice—fantastic," she replied. "And do you know why?"

"No, why?"

"Because this morning I interviewed the mayor."

"The mayor?"

"That's right. I told him about Maggie. By the way, have you seen Maggie today?"

"No, I have not. She is not inside sleeping?"

"No, I don't think so."

Maurice went over to the cardboard house and began hitting it with his knuckles. "Maggie?" he called. "You in there, Maggie?" He shrugged his shoulders as he looked back to Della. "Guess not," he said. "So, what were you saying about the mayor?"

"Well, like I said, I interviewed the mayor this morning. I told him that I was doing an article on the homeless. And I also told him about Maggie, and I asked him a lot of questions about the city's clean-up campaign."

"And what did he have to say about all that?"

"Well, let's just put it this way. After I got through with him, he shuffled his priorities around. It took a little convincing, but I finally got him to postpone his big plans for a while."

"That is magnificent," Maurice said, his voice glazed with excitement. "But how did you do that?"

"It was actually very simple. The mayor knows that my story could make him look very bad, just from the sympathetic angle that I could use. You know—big, bad, bully mayor—poor, defenseless little lady. It certainly wouldn't be very good public relations."

"So then Maggie does not have to leave?"

"For now, Maurice—for now. What it means is that everything is on hold. But after my story goes into print, I would bet a dollar to a donut, the mayor's big plans will just fly away like an eagle."

"That would be magnificent."

"Yes, it would."

"When Maggie hears about this, she will be so happy."

"Yes, she will. I wonder where she is."

"I do not know," he said. A thought suddenly occurred to him. "By the way, did she tell you that her birthday is coming up?"

"No, she never said anything to me. When is it?"

"Oh, not for another six weeks. Please, do not say anything to her, but I am going to make her a beautiful birthday cake. It will be so magnificent."

"That's nice of you. And don't worry, I won't say a thing."

"Merci beaucoup."

"You know, Maurice, I've got to tell you something that's—well—well, it's kind of strange, that's all."

"What is it?"

"Nothing really, I guess. It's just that I'm about the same age that Maggie's daughter would be right now. Kind of a coincidence, isn't it?"

"Oui, it is very much a coincidence."

"I guess stranger things have happened."

"Oui, and I am living proof of that."

"What do you mean?"

"Oh, I do not want to bore you with my story."

"No, please, I'd like to hear your story."

"Oui?"

"Oui."

Maurice funneled memories from his heart and soul, capturing images of his family, his friends, and the land where he grew up. "When I was a little boy, growing up in France, in Bordeaux, I would bake whenever I could do so. It started with one loaf of bread. My mother taught me how. From that first loaf of bread, I knew that I had found something tres bon. We had a small farm, and there were chores to do, but I grew up with two brothers and two sisters, so that gave me more time to do my baking.

"I would make bread and pastries, and I would give them to everyone. In return, they would give me things too, like eggs and milk, and chickens, and jellies, and candy, and even books, and sometimes, even money. But I never asked for anything in return. If they would insist, I would take it."

Della found herself drawn into Maurice's story. The smile that had settled upon his face grew a little as he thought of a very special person from his past.

"There was an old man who lived by himself in a little house," he continued, "farther away than anyone else that we knew. He was a lonely widower. He did not say very much to anyone, and people did not say very much to him. Some people called him a hermit. His name was Monsieur Cousteau. I called him by his first name—Pierre.

"We would play chess, and he would tell me stories. He was a very nice man, but a very lonely man. He was the only one who would never give me anything in return for my breads and pastries. But I did not care, because I knew he enjoyed my company, and I enjoyed his."

As he continued, Della drew images from his story, and she found herself eager for every word that he spoke.

"I grew up with a dream to have my own bakery," he continued, "and when I was eleven, I thought maybe that is all it would ever be—just a dream. Then one day, my friend Pierre, he died, and he left me a box.

"Inside the box was a letter thanking me for my friendship, and along with it was a lot of money that he had left for me. You see, I was his only friend. In the letter, he said that if it were not for me, he would have died of loneliness instead of old age.

"So I took my money and came to the United States of America and opened up my bakery. My dream had come true."

Della had been deeply moved by Maurice's story. "That's a beautiful story, Maurice," she said.

"Oui. But now I must go. I must get over to the bakery. I will be seeing you later."

"Okay, Maurice. It was nice talking to you. And thank you for sharing your story with me."

"Oui, it was my pleasure. I must go now."

"Have a nice day, Maurice."

"Merci, and you too."

He took a few steps away, but then turned back around and came back to Della. "Uh, Della…"

"Yes?"

"I was, uh—I was uh, kind of wondering if you would like to have dinner with me tonight?"

There were unmistakable sparkles in her eyes as she answered him with a glowing smile. "I'd love to have dinner with you," she said.

"Magnificent."

"You know, I wasn't suppose to say anything, but Maggie told me that you asked her if I was married or had a boyfriend."

Maurice was truly embarrassed. "She did?" he replied. "How embarrassing."

"You don't have to be embarrassed. You see, I asked her about you, too."

"You did? She did not say anything to me."

"She wasn't supposed to."

"Just like she was not supposed to tell you what I said."

They shared a bit of laughter. But the humor was replaced with serious expressions. They looked deeply into each other's eyes, and shimmering affection went dancing all the way to each other's heart. Della managed to turn her attention to her purse. She reached inside and removed a small tablet and a pen.

"I'll write down my address and phone number for you," she said.

"That would be magnificent."

Della wrote down the information and tore the piece of paper out of the tablet. "Here you go," she said, handing it to him.

"Merci. I will pick you up at seven-thirty. Okay?"

"That's fine."

"I will see you tonight," he said.

"See you tonight."

Suddenly they noticed Maggie approaching them from the east side of the alley. She was carrying a sack of potatoes, and she had a big, warm smile on her face.

"Bonjour, Maggie."

"Hi, Maggie," Della greeted. "Where've you been?"

"I took some cans into the recycling place," she explained. "Then I bought these potatoes." She put the sack of potatoes on the card table.

"Maggie, I have something for you." Della removed an envelope from her purse. "Here you go," she said, handing it to her.

"What's this?" Maggie asked, taking the envelope.

"Open it, and you'll find out."

Maggie opened the envelope and removed the letter. Della and Maurice waited anxiously for her to read it. She read it silently, then with excitement ringing in her voice, she yelled out, "I don't have to leave!"

"Now, Maggie, it's only temporary," Della reminded her.

"But there is a chance that you might not ever have to leave," Maurice added. "Right, Della?" he asked to confirm.

"Well, yes, there is a chance."

"What made the mayor do this?" Maggie asked.

Maurice spoke in a proud tone of voice. "Della, that is who," he said. "You can thank her for talking to him."

"I don't know what to say, except, well, just thank you."

"The pleasure was mine."

Maggie focused her attention on Della. "I can hardly wait till ol' Fuzzball McGuinness hears about this," she said.

Suddenly, there he was—Officer McGuinness, approaching them, his feet drumming a firm rhythm with each step of the way. There was a cold, calculated gaze in his eyes that matched the stern expression plastered upon his determined face.

"Well, look who's here—McFuzzball himself."

"We were just talking about you," Maurice said.

Officer McGuinness gave Maggie a long, intimidating stare. He made a point to deliver his message slowly and clearly. "Maggie, you've got until tomorrow," he said, "then I am going to take all this mess and throw it in the dumpster. Understand?"

"When roosters lay eggs!" she snapped. Then she handed him the letter. "Read it and weep, McFuzzball."

His face wrinkled with disbelief as he read the letter, and his expression quickly became flushed with anger. "How did this happen?" he asked. "I wasn't told anything at all about this. I just don't understand it. What is going on here? How did this happen?"

Della looked at Maggie and Maurice. "We don't have any idea, do we?" she asked.

"No," they answered together.

Officer McGuinness gave a cold, suspecting look to Della. "You had something to do with this, didn't you," he asked.

"Me?" she answered innocently. "Well of course not."

"Don't lie to me, Miss Priss."

"Who do you think you are, calling me Miss Priss?"

Maurice was quick to defend her. "Oui," he said, "who do you think you are?"

"My name is not Miss Priss," Della said.

"Yeah, you tell him, Fancy Pants," Maggie added.

That brought a laugh from Officer McGuinness. "Oh yeah, that's right," he teased, "it's Fancy Pants, isn't it?"

"No, it is not."

He squinted his eyes and gave a strong, threatening stare to Della and Maurice. "Look, I'm warning you both," he said, "don't interfere with police business."

What are you going to do—arrest us?" Della asked.

"If I have to."

"On what charge?"

"Interfering with a police officer."

"That's a line of crap, McFuzzball, and you know it." Maggie replied sharply.

"Oui," Maurice added. "This is police harassment."

"I think you all better have a little more respect for the law," the officer warned.

"Oh, we do have respect for the law," Della explained, "and for all the other police officers in this city. We just don't have any respect for you. How can we?"

Frustration was boiling inside the officer. He shot one last threatening stare to Maggie. "Enjoy it while you can, Maggie," he reminded her. "It's only temporary." Then he quickly walked away. As he headed for the west end of the alley, they all shared some laughter.

Maggie began dancing around, singing the *Dancing With Daffodil* song as her extended arms held onto Daffodil. Maggie smiled down at the child whom only she could see.

> *"Go and get your little red shoes,*
> *Dancing with Daffodil,*
> *Forget about your little-girl blues,*
> *Dancing with Daffodil.*
>
> *"Dance, dance, dance,*
> *Dancing with Daffodil,*
> *Dance, dance, dance,*
> *Dancing with Daffodil.*
>
> *"We'll dance and dance around and around,*
> *Dancing with Daffodil,*
> *We'll dance until the stars fall down,*
> *Dancing with Daffodil.*
>
> *"Dance, dance, dance,*
> *Dancing with Daffodil,*
> *Dance, dance, dance,*
> *Dancing with Daffodil."*

Instead of finishing the entire song, Maggie went back into her cardboard house.

"I have never met anyone like Maggie," Maurice said.

"Neither have I. That's such a pretty song that she always sings."

"Oui, and you can tell that it has so much meaning for her."

"Yes, I know. The way she dances around with that expression on her face, and the way she pretends that she's dancing with her daughter—it's so—so—well, I can only imagine what she's feeling."

"Oui, I can almost imagine her daughter—her little Daffodil dancing with her."

"I know, me too. I keep thinking about all the guilt and loneliness she's had to live with."

"And then to live here, like this," he said.

"And that cop is only trying to make things worse."

"Oui, he is a very mean man."

"Well, he better just lay off. For now, Maggie has the right to be here."

"I just hope the mayor lets her stay for as long as she wants," he said.

"Yes, that would be nice."

"Well, I guess maybe I better go now," he said, moving closer to her. "I will see you tonight, Della."

Della felt herself being pulled into his dreamy stare, and she anticipated what might follow. Her heart began to beat a little faster. "Okay," she said, "see you tonight, Maurice." The passion that pulsed in their hearts was echoed in the sparkles dancing in their eyes. They embraced each other and met in a tender kiss.

Maggie popped her head out of the cardboard house and conveyed a teasing smile to Della and Maurice. "Ooh, la la," she teased, "Frenchy and Fancy Pants."

"His first love of baking had become his second love, for Della had definitely become his first."

CHAPTER FIVE

During the month that had passed by, Maurice and Della had spent a great deal of time together falling in love. Officer McGuinness was busy trying to find some way to get Maggie out of the alley. There was another collection of cans saved up in a bag next to a shopping cart, and everything else looked the same as it did a month before.

Maurice had just left the bakery. Although he was on his way to see Maggie, his thoughts were on Della, and he was thinking deeply with his heart. His first love of baking had become his second love, for Della had definitely become his first. But neither Maurice nor Della had actually conveyed their love with the exact three little words.

Officer McGuinness wore an evil smile upon his face as he walked down the busy street. He had an idea, and he made it work for him. In his own twisted way, he was proud of himself for accomplishing such a sinister task. He made his way down the alley, passing the garbage cans, the dumpsters, and the graffiti. When he had arrived at the sight that he had come to know so well, the sight that had been torturing his soul, he stopped and just stared. The nefarious twitch in his eyes focused on the cardboard house, and a mischievous smile grew upon his face.

He began beating on the cardboard house with his nightstick. "Come on out of there, Maggie!" he yelled. He continued to strike the cardboard house. "Come on," he said. "Crawl out of there like you always do—like a snake." He began laughing. "Just like a hobo snake," he continued, taunting with great pleasure, beating on the house. "Maggie, I know you're in there! Now damn it, come out!"

A ball of fire rolled through Maurice as he arrived and witnessed Officer McGuinness beating on the cardboard house. There was a tone of shock in his voice. "What are you doing?" he asked.

Officer McGuinness stopped the beating and turned to answer him. "I'm trying to get this stubborn hobo woman to come out of this cardboard piece of crap!" he said.

A look of disbelief was sustained on Maurice's face. "You ought to be ashamed of yourself," he said.

"Look, Maurice, I don't tell you how to make your donuts, so don't tell me how to do *my* job."

"It is not your job, or anybody else's job, to go around terrorizing people. And by the way, Maggie is not here."

"Yeah, well where is she?"

"I do not think that is any of your business."

"Oh yeah?" Well, just in case you haven't noticed, Mr. Baker Man, I just happen to be an officer of the law. And let me tell you something. I don't think it would be very wise to interfere with the law."

"Excusez-moi, but I do not look at you as being an officer of the law. You are no more than a bully."

Officer McGuinness began waving the nightstick at him. "You just better be careful of what you say to me, Mr. Baker Man. Instead of poking holes in donuts, you'll be poking your head through bars."

"I have done nothing wrong," Maurice said. "I am only speaking the truth. And I am not Mr. Baker Man! My name is Maurice—Maurice Bonné."

"Yeah, well your name is going to be shit if you don't watch your step! I mean it, Maurice. If you don't show a little more respect for me, I'll haul your ass off to jail."

"You cannot threaten me," Maurice said. "I know my rights. I am an American citizen," he continued proudly. "I came to this country to see my dream come true. I know my rights. You cannot haul my ass, or any other part of my body, off to jail. I am an American, and I am entitled to liberty." Maurice felt good about what he had just said. He felt proud.

"Yeah, well you break the law, and there'll be no more liberty for you."

"I respect the laws, and you cannot tell me that I have broken any, can you?"

"Not yet."

"Has Maggie broken the law?"

"No, not yet."

"Then why don't you just leave her alone? Quit harassing her."

Officer McGuinness focused his cruel, intimidating eyes on Maurice and shook the nightstick at him. "Don't you tell me what to do," he said sternly. "I'll do whatever I want. And I'm warning you, I'll make sure that I find something that will send your French ass to jail. And the same thing goes for your hobo friend."

Maurice snapped back quickly to defend Maggie. "She has done nothing wrong. You leave her alone."

"Where's she at, Maurice?"

"Je né sais pas."

"What the hell does that mean?"

"It means I do not know."

"Yeah, well I think you're lying. Now I'm going to ask you one more time, and you better tell me the truth. Where is she?"

Overwhelmed by the officer's intimidation, Maurice capitulated. "I saw her this morning when she was leaving," he admitted. "She just said that she was going to see a friend."

"A friend? She's a damn hobo. She doesn't have any friends."

Maurice began to feel brave again, brave enough to shoot words of anger from his heart in an effort to defend Maggie. "I am sure that she has more friends than you have," he said, "that is if you have any friends at all."

"Yeah, well she and all her trampy trash are getting run out of the city. We're cleaning up this mess from top to bottom."

"You are a very cruel man, McGuinness."

"That's *Officer* McGuinness," he corrected.

"I do not think you know this, but two weeks from today is Maggie's birthday. So why don't you just quit harassing her? That would make a real nice early birthday gift."

"I've got a gift for her, all right," he replied. He pulled out an envelope from his pocket. "It's right here in this envelope," he boasted, "only the gift isn't from me. It's from the chief of police."

"Like I said, you are a very cruel man—a very selfish man."

"Shouldn't you be poking holes in your donuts, Maurice?"

"Should you not be out protecting the public from criminals, McGuinness?"

"That's *Officer* McGuinness."

Maurice felt pushed to the limit, and he began to shoot back with a cannon of emotions. "You are a disgrace to the respectable police department we have here in this city," he said. "I guess there is always one bad apple."

"You just watch your step, Maurice, or I'll show you just how bad this apple can be."

"I am tired of your threats. I am going to report this to the chief of police."

"You say anything at all, and I promise you, I'll make sure that life will be pure hell for Maggie. Do you understand me?"

"The only thing I understand is that you have pushed me and Maggie too far," Maurice replied.

"Just remember what I said. You say anything to anybody, and I'll make sure that you and Maggie are breaking the law, then you'll both be hauled off to jail."

"You do not scare me, McGuinness."

"That's *Officer* McGuinness."

"After I tell the chief of police what you have said, maybe you will not be an officer any more."

The officer's eyes were focused and cold, his face frozen with a threatening expression. "You better just keep your mouth shut, Maurice, if you know what's good for you, and if you know what's good for that hobo friend of yours," he warned.

"I know what is good for me, and you better not do anything to hurt Maggie."

"Tell me something, Mr. Baker Man. Whatever happened to that reporter, or whatever the hell she is?"

"I do not think that is any of your business," Maurice replied.

"She's probably been writing her precious story about the bums of this city."

Suddenly, they both noticed Maggie coming down the alley. Officer McGuinness was anxious to give Maggie the letter, and it showed on his face, augmenting the irritation that Maurice already felt.

"Hi, Frenchy," she said, approaching them.

"Bonjour, Maggie."

Maggie gave Officer McGuinness a stare of disgust. "What are you doing here, McGuinness?" she asked.

"That's *Officer* McGuinness," he replied.

"You mean *Fuzzball* McGuinness," she snapped.

He was now a fox who had cornered his prey, and there was an obvious tone of mischief in his voice. "I understand that you've got a birthday coming up in about two weeks," he said.

She looked at Maurice. "Did you tell him?" she asked.

"Oui."

"I brought you an early birthday present," Officer McGuinness said. He handed the envelope to Maggie.

"What's this?" she asked.

"Well, let's see—what were the words you used? Oh, yes. I remember now. Read it and weep."

Maggie opened the envelope and removed the letter. She read it silently as Maurice looked and waited with curiosity. "No way!" she said. "No way! No way!"

Officer McGuinness replied with aggravating laughter.

Maggie was furious. "McGuinness, you freakin' fuzzball! How did you get the mayor to change his mind?"

"I had nothing to do with it," he lied. "Besides, you knew he was only letting you stay here on a temporary basis."

Maggie's words tore back at him with a clear, stern tone. "I'm not going anywhere," she said.

"That's where you're wrong, Maggie. I'm getting you out of here right now."

"Oh no you're not," she snapped.

"Oh yes I am."

Maurice had been quiet up to now, just listening and observing. But he knew it was time to do whatever it took to help Maggie. His face was flushed with anger. "Leave her alone!" he said, his voice loud and stern.

"Leave her alone?" Officer McGuinness replied. "Leave her alone?" Painful images from the past flashed in his mind. "It was a bum just like her that killed my partner. Did you know that? No, you didn't know that, did you?" Then he looked at Maggie, the chip on his shoulder inflamed by his confrontation with her. "And neither did you, did you?" he asked. "Well, it's true."

Maggie and Maurice were silent as Officer McGuinness looked at both of them to make sure that he had a captivated audience. "One night my partner and I were chasing a guy who just robbed a store and shot a clerk. We chased him right into this alley—right here in this damn alley." He pointed to the area behind the chinese restaurant. "Then, just right down there behind Eddie Chan's, that guy snuck up behind my partner and aimed his gun at him.

"I had a clear shot at that bastard, but some other bastard got in the way. It was a lousy, drunk bum. He just walked right out into the line of fire. I yelled at him, and I yelled at my partner, but it was too late. By the time I fired, the suspect had already shot and killed my partner before taking a fatal bullet himself. My partner died in the line of duty, and it was all because of that lousy, drunk hobo." He gave Maggie a cold, evil look. "So you see, Maggie, bums like you don't belong in this alley."

"I think you just need to get rid of that chip on your shoulder, McGuinness," Maggie said.

"Oui, what happened to your partner has nothing to do with Maggie," Maurice added.

"It has everything to do with Maggie!" he replied. "And now I'm going to get her out of this alley." His voice filled the alley as he focused his attention to Maggie. "You're leaving, Maggie, right now! And I mean right now!"

"Oh no I'm not!"

"Oh yes you are!"

"This is very wrong," Maurice said. "You cannot do this."

"Oh yeah? Watch me!" He began throwing things into the shopping cart.

"You freakin' fuzzball!" Maggie shouted. "What are you doing? Leave my stuff alone!"

"All this crap is going in the dumpster!" Officer McGuinness yelled back.

"No! No, that's my property!"

Maurice began taking the items out of the shopping cart. "Stop it!" he yelled. "Damn it, you leave her stuff alone!"

Maurice was filled with anger as he got in front of the officer. He tried to stop him from throwing her possessions into the shopping cart, blocking the cart with his hands. Pushing and shoving quickly turned into a struggle, and Officer McGuinness knocked Maurice to the ground.

"You crazy French bastard!" Officer McGuinness screamed at him. "Get out of my way or I'll beat the crap out of you!"

Maurice managed to get up again. "Stop it!" he yelled. "Damn it, stop it! Stop it! Stop it!" He looked at Maggie and saw that she was shaking with fear.

Officer McGuinness began waving his nightstick around. He was out of control, and the expression upon his face was one of madness. With a rage of insanity, he focused in on Maggie. "Say good-bye to your cardboard condo!" he screamed. Then he began beating on the cardboard house.

Maggie and Maurice were both yelling at him, both of them terrorized at the hands of the officer. They were yelling, "No! Stop it! Stop it!"

Maurice gathered up all the strength he had to physically stop Officer McGuinness from destroying Maggie's house. There was grabbing, pushing, shoving. He tried everything he could think of. "Stop it, damn it!" he yelled. "You leave Maggie's house alone!" The struggle finally ended with Officer McGuinness beating Maurice with the nightstick.

Maggie was screaming, her whole body shaking with terror. Maurice fought with every bit of strength he had, but he was knocked to the ground again, and Officer McGuinness continued to beat him. The sight of Maurice in agony, the blood on his head, body, and clothes drove Maggie to become hysterical and helpless, her mind pulsing with shock, her heart beating with intense fear, her tears streaming down her face. She cried out with sustaining screams, and she watched in horror as Maurice's eyes closed. His bloodied head fell, and he became unconscious.

"Both of you ought to be run out of this town!" Officer McGuinness said. "You've got no respect for the law! Absolutely no respect!"

"Oh, my God!" Maggie yelled. "Oh, my God! I think you've killed him! Oh, my God! I think you've killed him!"

Officer McGuinness just looked down at his victim, and smiled insanely. "I wouldn't worry about that," he said. "You can't kill a French bastard like him." Then he broke out in aggravating laughter. "Just to show you what a nice guy I am," he continued, "I'll give you until Monday to get out of here. But that's it. I'll be back Monday, and you and all your crap better be gone. Because if not, then you're going to jail!"

Trembling with fear, she stared at the sadistic grin of satisfaction that swept over his face. "You son of a bitchin' monster!" She screamed. "You bastard!"

Officer McGuinness responded by striking Maggie with his nightstick, and she yelled out with horrible pain as she fell to the ground.

He looked down at her with his cruel eyes. "Hobo bitch!" he yelled. "Damn, stinkin' hobo bitch!"

As Maggie knelt down next to Maurice, her face filled with terror, Officer McGuinness walked away, gazing back with one last nefarious grin. Through her tear-filled eyes, she looked at Maurice. He was still unconscious. "Oh, my God," she said. "Frenchy. Frenchy. No. No. Frenchy, wake up. Please wake up. No. No, please God. Frenchy, please wake up. Oh, my God." But he didn't respond. He didn't wake up.

**"Her feet became still,
her voice silent,
her hands empty,
her heart filled
with painful memories."**

CHAPTER SIX

Two weeks had passed by, and it was early afternoon in the city. Birds played in Golden Gate Park, fluttering their wings, singing their songs, and gliding down to the trees and green carpet below. There were people strolling through the park. From lovers who were sharing the day with each other, to those lonely people who shared the past with themselves, to those who were sitting on a park bench, having their lunch or feeding the birds, every soul was influenced by the ambience of that beautiful spring day.

Sea gulls soared along the beaches, and the animals in the zoo seemed to move with a little more spirit than usual. Some businessmen who normally walked quickly throughout the financial district without a smile had slowed their pace while relinquishing an occasional smile at people, cars, and even the towers of glass and steel surrounding them.

Near Market Street, more light than usual spilled into the alley that was home to Maggie May Salokavich. Near the cardboard house was a bag that held another collection of empty cans.

Maggie came out of her house and picked up a wine bottle filled with water. There was a bright smile on her face as she began watering her King Alfred daffodils, pouring the water into the flower pot.

"Here you go, Alfred," she said to one of the beautiful yellow flowers. "Oh, I'm sorry, Your Highness. I mean *King* Alfred. Don't worry, it's just water." She continued to pour the water into the flower pot, and address each of the flowers. "And some for you, King Alfred, and for you, King Alfred, and for you, King Alfred. My goodness, so many kings in one flower pot. Whoops, did I say flower pot? I'm sorry, Your Highnesses. I mean kingdom—so many kings in one kingdom, of course. So many kings—so many Alfreds—so much royalty. And you're all so very handsome—such handsome kings." A thought suddenly occurred to her, and she was eager to share it. "Oh, you know what?" she said. "I found my Queen Anne bulbs, so next year, my beautiful Queen Annes will be blooming just like you guys."

As she continued to pour water into the flower pot, she thought about what had happened just two weeks ago in the alley. She thought about the attack, and she thought about how lucky she and Maurice were, because their injuries could have been worse, and how it had all changed her situation.

She continued to talk to her King Alfred daffodils. "You know," she said, as if they could understand every word she was saying, "it sure is wonderful that we don't have to leave the alley now. Of course, it took for me and Frenchy to get beat up. But that will never happen again, because that ol' Fuzzball McGuinness won't be around for a while. He's going to be walking his beat in a cell."

She looked directly at one of the daffodils as if it could look back at her. "He should have known you can't go around harassing and hurting people like that," she said. "And forging the chief of police's signature on that stolen letterhead—that wasn't too bright either."

She turned her focus to another flower. "Well, at least I got a formal letter of apology from the mayor and the chief of police," she boasted. "I still can't get over how they both showed up that day, right here, just to apologize to me personally."

Thoughts of the brutal behavior by Officer McGuinness haunted Maggie's mind. She poured a little more water into the pot. "I'll never forget what McGuinness did to me and Frenchy," she said, glancing at the daffodils. Images of terror flashed before her. "I thought for sure that he had killed Frenchy," she said, focusing in on one of the King Alfreds. "I'll never forget how he looked, lying there on the ground, unconscious, bleeding. But he's okay now, and that's all that matters. He's out of the hospital and back to making all those tasty treats at his bakery."

A thought entered her mind, and as she spoke, she made sure that her eyes were on all of the daffodils. "By the way, do you know what day this is?" she asked. "It's my birthday, and I feel especially fortunate." She then began to stare into space. "I can be very thankful on this birthday, because I have survived. I have survived the cold, and the hunger, and I have survived that ol' Fuzzball McGuinness." Then she seemed to be overcome by a wave of sadness sweeping over her face. "But most of all," she continued, "I have survived the heart-breaking loneliness of Daffodil and her mother being separated for all these years."

She extended her arms and held out her hands to the imaginary little girl. She began dancing with Daffodil while singing that song most dear to her heart. But as she danced, as she sang, and as she gazed down at the imaginary little girl, the smile that would normally be on her face could not break through the expression of sadness.

"Go and get your little red shoes,
Dancing with Daffodil,
Forget about your little-girl blues,
Dancing with Daffodil.

"Dance, dance, dance,
Dancing with Daffodil,
Dance, dance, dance,
Dancing with Daffodil.

"We'll dance and dance around and around,
Dancing with Daffodil,
We'll dance until the stars fall down,
Dancing with Daffodil."

Maggie was overcome by tears flooding her eyes, but she tried to continue while she cried. Her words became broken and slurred.

"Dance, dance,--dance,
Dancing with Daf..."

She was now completely overtaken by her emotions. Her feet became still, her voice silent, her hands empty, her heart filled with painful memories. As she dried her eyes and tried to compose herself, she noticed a familiar face approaching. It was Maurice. He was carrying a boxed birthday cake.

As Maurice came closer, he realized that Maggie was upset. "Oh, dear," he said as he walked up to her, "you have been crying? Are you okay?"

"I'm fine, Frenchy," she replied. "Don't worry about it. Crying is good for the soul."

"Well, happy birthday, Maggie. I baked you a cake."

"Oh, Frenchy, thank you. How nice of you."

"Making you a cake is the least I can do for such a wonderful lady on her birthday."

"Frenchy, you are such a wonderful guy—with the exception of my husband, the most wonderful guy I have ever met."

"Merci beaucoup. That means a lot to me." He put the cake on the table and opened the box.

Maggie took a good, long look at the cake. "Happy birthday, Maggie" she read out loud. "It's beautiful."

"I am happy that you like it. Excuse me for a minute. I have got something else for you. I left it with Eddie Chan. I will be right back." He quickly walked away, heading toward Eddie Chan's Chinese Restaurant.

"How about that," she said to herself, "a birthday cake, for *me*."

As she turned toward the opposite end of the alley, Maggie noticed Della approaching in the near distance. Carrying a full grocery bag and a wrapped birthday gift, Della greeted her with a smile.

"Della!" Maggie said with surprise.

"Happy birthday, Maggie," Della replied. Then she handed Maggie the gift.

"For me? Another gift, for me?"

"You can't open it yet. Okay?"

"Okay. What's in the bag?"

"Oh, just some plates and napkins, and cups and soda, and a few other items."

Maggie's voice was glazed with obvious excitement. "This is just like a party," she said.

"It is a party. Come on, let's get things ready." She noticed the cake on the table. "Oh, what a beautiful cake."

"Maurice made it for me," Maggie replied proudly.

"I know. He told me he was going to make you a cake."

"He just went down to Eddie Chan's," Maggie said. "He said he'd be right back." She spoke her feelings without hesitation. "He's such a nice guy."

Maggie's comment brought an obvious smile to Della's face, echoing her feelings for Maurice. "He sure is," she replied—"a *very* nice guy."

"You're in love with him, aren't you?"

"Yes, I am."

"He loves you, too. He told me so."

"He did?"

"He sure did."

"Come on, lift up your cake, and I'll put the table cloth on the table."

"Okay."

Maggie lifted the cake, and Della took the tablecloth out of the grocery bag and put it on the table. Maggie put the cake back down, and Della reached into the bag and removed the paper cups and plates, napkins, plastic utensils, and the soda. She put everything on the table as if each item had a special place where it had to be.

"I've got a big surprise for you, Maggie."

"This is surprise enough," Maggie said.

Maurice had a big smile on his face as he returned from Eddie Chan's Chinese Restaurant. He was carrying a wrapped gift.

"Hi, Maurice," Della said.

"Bonjour, Della." He put the gift on the table.

Della glanced at the table. "As you can see," she said proudly, "I've got the table all fixed."

"C'est bon."

"Maggie, I'd like you to open my gift," Della said.

"Open your gift? Aren't we supposed to have cake first? Aren't you supposed to sing Happy Birthday to me? Aren't I supposed to make a wish?"

Della quickly gave her an assuring smile. "Believe me," she said, "there's a reason that all of this is backwards. You see, we're expecting a very special guest."

"A special guest? Who?"

"Well, that's going to be your big surprise. And that guest is waiting not too far from here. But before that guest can join us, you need to open the gift from me."

"I never had a birthday like this one before."

Della handed the wrapped gift to Maggie. "Here, Maggie," she said, "open this."

"I feel like I'm in a dream," she said, taking the gift. She unwrapped it and slid the top of the box away. As she pulled back the tissue paper, a beautiful red dress came into view. She was overwhelmed and momentarily speechless as she took the dress out of the box and gazed at it. "A dress. It's—it's—it's so beautiful. This is for me?"

"Well, it's not for me," Della said.

"And certainly it is not for me," Maurice joked.

"Maggie, I think you should try it on," Della suggested.

"But it's much too beautiful for me to wear."

"Don't be ridiculous, Maggie. If anything, you're much too beautiful for the dress. Now go try it on. You can use the restroom at Eddie Chan's."

"Oui. As a matter of fact, Eddie is expecting you. He has a gift for you."

"Really? Another gift for me?"

"Oui."

"So go down there and put on the dress," Della insisted.

"Okay. I'll be right back." She walked away and headed for Eddie Chan's Chinese Restaurant.

"This is working out just fine," Maurice said.

"Yes, it is."

"She is going to be so surprised."

"I know," Della agreed. "I just keep wondering how she's going to react."

"I know what you mean, but I think it will be okay. I think everything will be just fine."

"I hope so."

"It will," he assured her.

Della looked at him with concern. "I just hope she doesn't see her surprise when she's in Eddie Chan's restaurant," she said.

"Don't worry about that. Eddie is keeping her in a private room. Besides that, she is in—in—how do you say that?"

"Incognita," Della answered. "That's true, she is."

"You know, Della, I am going to miss her. I am going to miss her very much."

"I imagine you will. I haven't known her as long as you have, but I'm going to miss her, too. Of course, who knows? Maybe she'll stay right here in San Francisco."

"That would be nice, but I do not think so."

"It's ironic, isn't it?" she said. "I mean how we fought so hard to keep her right here, right here where she wanted to be, and now…"

"And now we have sent her away," he finished.

"Yes, but her whole life is going to turn around again, this time in a good way."

"It will be like a miracle for her," he said.

"Yeah, I guess it will."

He looked at her proudly. "If you would have never come down here, she would have almost certainly spent the rest of her life without any hope."

Tiny sparkles were dancing in Della's eyes as she thought about how much Maurice meant to her. "And if I hadn't come down here," she replied, "most likely I would have never met you."

"But you did, and I am so happy that you did. I am happy for them, and I am happy for us."

"Me, too."

"You know, Della, I still do not understand why—well, you know."

"Yeah, I don't understand it either, Maurice. Maybe we can make some sense of it in a little while."

"Oui, I certainly hope so."

She had a silly grin on her face. "It should be interesting," she said.

He moved closer to her and looked deeply into her eyes. "It is a wonderful thing that you have done," he said.

"I didn't do anything Maurice. It was just fate, that's all."

Maggie had just put her new dress on. Normally there was only the small mirror on the wall, but Eddie Chan had brought a full-length mirror from home just so Maggie could take a good look at herself in the dress. It was his idea. He had even provided the shampoo that she had used to wash her now clean hair.

As she ran a hairbrush through her hair, she looked into the mirror at the beautiful red dress. With a silly grin, she lifted her gaze, put the hairbrush down, and stared into her own proud eyes. "Maggie May Salokavich," she said to her reflection, "what a beautiful dress you have on."

She slipped into the images of the past. Her arms extended outward with the palms of her hands open. She closed her hands as she clutched onto the imaginary hands. Then she began to dance her dance and sing her song as she gazed down at the imaginary child.

"Go and get your little red shoes,
Dancing with Daffodil,
Forget about your little-girl blues,
Dancing with Daffodil."

A woman entered the restroom and just stood there momentarily while Maggie continued.

"Dance, dance, dance,

Dancing with Daffodil,
Dance, dance, dance,
Dancing with Daffodil."

"Are you okay?" the woman asked.

Maggie stopped and looked at the woman. "I'm wonderful," she replied. Then she glanced at her new dress. "Do you like my new dress?" she asked.

"Uh, yeah. Yeah, it's nice."

"Nice? It's better than nice. It's beautiful. My friend Della gave it to me for my birthday. Della and Frenchy—he's my other friend—anyway, they're both waiting for me right now because they're giving me a birthday party. Isn't that wonderful?"

"Yeah. Yeah, that's wonderful. Maybe you should get some coffee."

"Maybe you should mind your own business," Maggie said with a stern look upon her face.

The woman found herself speechless. Without saying anything, she just walked away to one of the stalls and locked herself in. From inside the stall, she could hear the continued song as Maggie began with the chorus, her hands clutching those of Daffodil, her eyes focused upon the imaginary child. The woman could see Maggie's feet sliding across the floor, keeping rhythm to the song.

"Dance, dance, dance,
Dancing with Daffodil,
Dance, dance, dance,
Dancing with Daffodil."

"Della, like Maurice,
watched with anxiety running wild,
and Maggie was overcome
with curiosity
as a strange silence
took over the moment."

CHAPTER SEVEN

"You know, I was wondering about something, Della," Maurice said. "What inspired you to be a writer?"

"You really want to know?"

"Oui, s'il vous plait."

"Okay, then," she said, "I'll tell you. I was twelve years old, in the seventh grade. One day, my English class went on a field trip to a retirement home. Our assignment was to write about our visit." Maurice had a look on his face that told her that she had a captured audience, and that made her feel good about telling the story. "While I was there," she continued, "I spent most of my time with one particular lady. Her name was Betty. She was so lonely. Her family didn't visit her very often. Anyway, it really broke my heart.

"After I turned in my assignment, I wrote a poem for Betty, and I brought it to her, and I read it for her. She loved it. I gave her the poem, and she showed it to her family. After that, her family began visiting her all the time. So did I. That's the way it was until the day she passed away. My writing brought happiness into the life of a very lonely lady. That's when I knew that I wanted to be a writer."

Maurice was emotionally moved by Della's story. "That is so magnificent," he said. "Now you have brought happiness once again."

"And so have you."

A proud smile played on his face. "We are very good together," he said.

"Yes, we certainly are."

They looked deeply into each other's eyes. His fingers brushed her cheek. Their hearts were racing, pulsating with anticipation and the love they felt for each other.

"Della," he said softly, "Je t'aime. Je t'aime beaucoup."

His words were music, reaching into her heart with a thousand violins. And dancing to the music were tiny ballerinas in her eyes. "I love you, too, Maurice," she replied. "I love you very much."

Tenderly, their lips met in a sweet kiss. Another sustaining kiss followed as the winds of passion grew stronger. Like those tiny ballerinas in her eyes, there were little dancers in her heart.

Maurice and Della were suddenly interrupted as Maggie approached them. She had two gift certificates in her hand. "Ooh, la la," she teased, "Frenchy and Fancy Pants."

Della gazed at Maggie's new dress. "Look at you," she said. "That looks so beautiful on you."

"Oui, Maggie, it certainly does," Maurice added.

"But it really is too beautiful for me to wear."

Della faked a scolding expression. "Maggie, you get that thought right out of your mind," she said. "Things are going to change for you."

"They already have."

"So what do you have there in your hand?" Della asked.

"Certificates. Eddie gave me two certificates. Each one's good for ten dollars at his restaurant."

"C'est bon," Maurice said. "That was very nice of him."

"Maggie, like I've already told you, there's somebody else that we've invited to your party," Della said.

"But who is it?"

"I will go get her," Maurice said. With the excitement of a child, he headed down the alley toward Eddie Chan's Chinese Restaurant.

"It's a woman?" Maggie asked, curiosity glazing her voice.

"Yes."

"Is she a friend of yours?"

"She's just someone who wanted to come to your party, and she has a very special gift for you."

"Gift? But she doesn't even know me. Something very strange is going on here."

"Trust me, Maggie."

"So are we going to have some cake soon?"

"Yes, soon."

"That's good, because all this excitement has made me very hungry."

Maurice chose to exit the restaurant by way of the back door, entering the alley. With him was the guest of honor for Maggie's birthday party. Her face was concealed with a silk scarf and a pair of sunglasses. She wore a plain, simple dress and shoes, and clutched in her hands was a wrapped gift the size of a shoe box.

Maurice and the woman continued down the alley, each deliberate step bringing with it an augmented degree of anxiety and anticipation. As they came close to their destination, their slow pace became even slower. Restricted by the flutter of butterflies, the heavy pounding of the heart, and images of another time flashing in her mind, the woman began to stall, and then she stopped. Maurice placed a comforting hand on her shoulder, and then they continued on, approaching their destination, which was now in full view.

With Maurice by her side, the woman walked slowly toward Maggie. Della, like Maurice, watched with anxiety running wild, and Maggie was overcome with curiosity as a strange silence took over the moment. As Maggie and the woman faced each other, Della and Maurice were left speechless.

"Happy birthday," the woman said, handing Maggie the gift. Her voice was gentle, soothing, and Maggie found it to be oddly familiar.

"You brought me a gift?" Maggie asked, glancing at the gift, then back to the woman.

"Yes, of course I did."

"But you don't even know me."

"But I *do* know you."

"You do? Maggie asked, surprised. "How? Who are you? I can't really see your face."

"Please," the woman insisted, "just open the gift."

"What's going on here?" Maggie asked, glancing at all of them.

"Go on, open it," Della said.

"Something very weird is going on here." Slowly, methodically, carefully, Maggie began to peel away the birthday paper. Then the surface of the shoe box was bare. With augmented caution, she lifted the lid, brushed aside the tissue paper and peered inside. Frozen with shock, she could hardly believe her eyes. Too overwhelmed by the sight, she could say nothing, not even a whisper as she reached into the box, her eyes never leaving the contents. Carefully, she lifted a pair of little red shoes out of the box. She gazed inside the shoes and silently read what had been written there, first the left one, and then the right.

She read the writing inside the right shoe again, this time out loud, her voice textured with surprise.

"Daffodil," she said. "Oh, my God. Where did you get these shoes?"

"Those were the last pair that you wore, just before they took you away from me," the woman replied. "And I didn't give any of them away like you said I did. I still have them all." She removed her silk scarf, and then her sunglasses. Their eyes were locked on each other. "My name is Maggie," the woman said, "Maggie May Salokavich. I'm your mother. Happy birthday, Daffodil. My sweet little Daffodil. My sweet little Daffodil. I thought I would never see you again. I lost all hope, but now here you are, after all these years."

Their eyes became flooded with tears as they embraced each other.

"Maggie, I mean Daffodil," Della explained, "your mother saw my story, and she contacted me right away. All this time, you were pretending to be your mother. All this time, you were actually Daffodil."

"But why?" Daffodil's mother asked. "Why, Daffodil? Why did you do that?"

"I don't know. I guess I just didn't want to be me anymore without you."

"I'm sorry, Daffodil. I'm sorry for what happened. I don't expect you to forgive me, but I want you to know that I have never stopped missing you. I've tried and tried to find you, but until I saw the magazine article, my search always took me to a dead end. I only hope that you can forgive me someday."

"At first I was so hurt," Daffodil explained, "and I was so afraid. Then I became so angry, but not just at those people who took me away. I was angry at *you*. I loved you, but I hated you for letting yourself become an alcoholic. I hated you for that. If you could have just controlled your drinking, they would have never taken me away from you."

"I know. I know, Daffodil, and I'm sorry. I'm so sorry. I didn't want them to take you away from me. It hurt me so much. It broke my heart, and I know it broke *your* heart. I caused a terrible thing to happen, and I've been paying for it ever since."

"I've been paying for it, too."

"I know you have. I can't bring back the past, Daffodil. All that I can say is that I'm sorry for what I caused to happen. And I know now that, even if they wouldn't have taken you away from me, life would have eventually been hell for you. I was sick, Daffodil, and I was getting sicker. I was an alcoholic, and I was a bad mother."

Daffodil's mother sobbed with guilt, tears flowing down her face. Daffodil embraced her. Then she looked at her mother with forgiving eyes. "You were a *good* mother," she said. "You were wonderful, until you started drinking so much. I'll never forget working with you in the garden. I'll never forget putting on my little red shoes, then dancing with you, and singing, and laughing."

"I won't either. I could never forget that. I'm so sorry, Daffodil."

Daffodil looked deeply into her mother's eyes. "I forgive you," she said.

"I don't deserve your forgiveness. I really don't. I love you."

"I love you, too."

"You know, Daffodil, I haven't touched a drink in a long time—ever since I got out of that clinic. And by the way, I never was in a mental hospital. It was a special clinic for the problem I had—

alcoholism. Although I did see a psychiatrist for a while."

"Oh, well, I wasn't really sure. All I remember is somebody telling me that you had to go to a special hospital."

Daffodil's mother managed to produce a smile. "My Daffodil," she said proudly. "My sweet little Daffodil." They embraced again, holding each other, feeling each other's pain. "How did you end up like this?" She asked. "How did you end up homeless?"

"Homeless? I'm not homeless." She pointed briefly to the cardboard house. "I've got my house right here."

"Here we go again," Della said.

"Oui," Maurice added, "here we go again."

"But I mean, how did you end up on the street?" Daffodil's mother asked again.

"Well, I was adopted by two very nice people. Then a few months later we moved to Nebraska. Then after I graduated from high school, I worked as a waitress and saved some money to come back to San Francisco.

"Right after my twentieth birthday, I came out here. I tried to find you. I looked everywhere. I went down to Watsonville, too. I looked all around the area—Santa Cruz, Gilroy, Hollister, Monterey, Salinas, Carmel, Pacific Grove, down to King City—all over."

"I had already moved to New York," her mother explained.

"New York? You mean New York City?"

"Yes, I went there to stay with an old friend. Anyway, I stayed with her for a while. Her husband died just a year before, so she enjoyed the company. It gave me time to get myself back together again—not completely, because I thought about you all the time. But anyway, I took some college courses, and I landed a real good job with a large corporation. So I did okay."

Della was about to burst with curiosity. "So how did you end up on the street?" she asked Daffodil.

"Oui," Maurice said. "I am also curious."

"Well, I met this guy, and we got married. Everything was going real good for almost eight years. Then he started drinking. Then he lost his job. Then we lost our house. We stayed with some friends for a while, but his drinking got way out of control. We got a divorce, then he ended up on the street. We didn't have any kids. We couldn't have any. Of course, the way things turned out, I guess that really was a blessing."

"My poor little Daffodil. You became a victim of alcoholism all over again."

"Yeah, I did. It was definitely a trip back to hell."

Maurice was quick to satisfy his curiosity. "So then how did you finally end up here—here on the streets?" he asked.

"I had a few waitress jobs, but my ex-husband would always harass me."

"Poor Maggie—I mean, Daffodil," Maurice said, "always getting harassed by someone."

"I'll say," Della added. "That's terrible."

"Yeah, so anyway," Daffodil continued, "that didn't work out. I mean it was really tough to hold a job. So, I finally ended up on the street, just like him. And that's where I stayed." She looked at her mother. Beams of truth left her eyes, and for a moment, she allowed the rest of the world to vanish. "And that's when I became you," she said. "I thought I would never find you, so instead of continuing to search for you, I just *became* you."

"Except this really is your birthday, Daffodil," her mother replied. "At least you didn't make *that* up."

"Yeah—forty-five years young, and you're—I don't even know how old you are."

"I'm sixty-eight."

"You both have been through so much," Della said.

Overwhelmed with guilt and thoughts of her daughter's misery, shame painted Maggie's face. "But Daffodil had to endure so much loneliness as a child, as well as an adult," she said.

"Yes, I did," Daffodil agreed. "It broke my heart when they took me away from you. It was so lonely without you. Then, when I was on the street for the first time, I felt like I was a child again—that same child who had been taken away from her mother. I was all by myself in the dark, in the cold, down by Fisherman's Wharf. I cried out for you so many times that night."

"Nobody should ever have to go through something like that," Della said.

"Oui, I can only imagine your misery."

"I'm sorry you had to go through all that hell," her mother said. "It's really all my fault."

"I don't want to talk about fault, or anything else that's bad," Daffodil replied. "I've had enough bad in my life, and so have you."

"That's for sure," her mother agreed.

"I think we should dance," Daffodil suggested. "Let's dance just like we used to."

"I don't have the music anymore. I accidentally destroyed the tape one night when I was drunk. I was so out of control that night, I destroyed everything in my path, even the extra copy."

"But we can still dance, can't we?"

There was a moment of syncopation before a smile swelled like a downbeat upon her mother's face. "Of course we can," she replied. "We can dance, and we can sing."

"Well, I would put on my little red shoes, but I don't think they would fit now."

Maurice handed his wrapped gift to Daffodil. "Here, Daffodil," he said. "I would like you to open my gift before you dance."

"Okay," she replied. She unwrapped the gift and opened it. Her eyes lit up as she gazed inside and took out a pair of red shoes. "Red shoes," she said.

"They are not quite the same as the ones you had when you were a little girl," he said, "but they are red shoes. And look inside."

She looked inside the shoes. "You put my name inside," she said with surprise.

"Oui, Maggie—I mean Daffodil."

"Thank you, Frenchy."

"You are welcome."

Daffodil took off her shoes and put on her new ones. "They fit perfectly," she said. "How did you know what size to get?"

"One day while you weren't here, I looked at a pair of your shoes," Della explained. "Then I told Maurice the size."

"I must confess, Della also helped me at the shoe store," he admitted.

"Thank you, Frenchy. You've been very special to me. Thanks for being such a great friend."

"The pleasure has been mine, Maggie—I mean Daffodil."

Daffodil and Maurice gave each other a warm hug. Then Daffodil went to Della. "Thank you, Della," she said. "Thank you for everything. If it weren't for you, my mother would have never found me. I probably would have never seen her again, and I would have never found my own self again." They too met in a warm embrace of friendship.

"I'm just glad I was able to help," Della said.

"Maurice, Della, you're the best friends I've ever had."

"You're an amazing lady—Daffodil," Della said.

"Oui, quite magnificent. And me and Della, we are going to miss you very much."

"Miss me?"

"But of course," Maurice replied. "I am sure you will be leaving here—I mean San Francisco."

There was an awkward silence that fell over them all. Maggie stepped closer to her daughter. In her heart, she felt the moment at hand had given her a chance to bring a special happiness into Daffodil's life. It would be a small token of happiness compared with the misery that she had endured, but it was something, possibly a new start. She looked at her daughter with a smile. "Would you like to stay here, Daffodil?"

"Of course I would, but I want to be with you, no matter what. That's the most important thing to me now—just for us to be together."

"I used to love this city," her mother said. "I still do. I'm going to move back here, and we can enjoy it together—again."

Maurice became filled with excitement. "Oh, c'est bon!" he said. "C'est bon! This is magnificent!"

"It sure is," Della added, trying her best to speak, and not to cry.

"I never thought that I'd ever feel this much happiness again," Daffodil said.

"Neither did I," her mother replied.

With a proud smile, Daffodil glanced down at her shoes. "Well, I've got my red shoes on," she said to her mother. "Shall we dance?"

"Yes, let's dance, Daffodil. Let's dance, and sing."

They extended their arms, their hands inviting the reunion. The emotions that surged when their fingers touched ran quickly to the heart, and to the soul. They began to dance and sing together.

"Go and get your little red shoes,
Dancing with Daffodil,
Forget about your little-girl blues,
Dancing with Daffodil.

"Dance, dance, dance,
Dancing with Daffodil,
Dance, Dance, Dance,
Dancing with Daffodil..."

Maurice and Della had joined them for a while, dancing in the style of the traditional waltz. When the last note had been sung, and the last step had been danced, Maurice and Della looked on proudly, basking in the glow of this glorious reunion of lost souls.

As Daffodil and her mother embraced, their hearts filled up with emotion, and for this mother and daughter, the strength of love and forgiveness could not have been stronger and sweeter.

"…Oh, right in broad daylight
in front of your eyes,
my wishes are flowin',
but I'm their disguise…."

From the song,
"Deep Down Low"
—Melanie Safka